The Lost Martian

Martian

Jesse Jimenez

Print information available on the last page

Rev. date: 03/24/2016

To order additional copies of this book, contact:
Xlibris
1-888-795-4274
www.Xlibris.com
Orders@Xlibris.com

The Lost
Martian

Jesse Jimenez

Once upon a time there was an astronaut named
Anthony. They called him the lost Martian.

Anthony did not look like a Martian from Mars so everyone would ask him why do they call you a Martian?

I am the flashing star in the sky he would say giggling. I went up into space with five other astronauts.

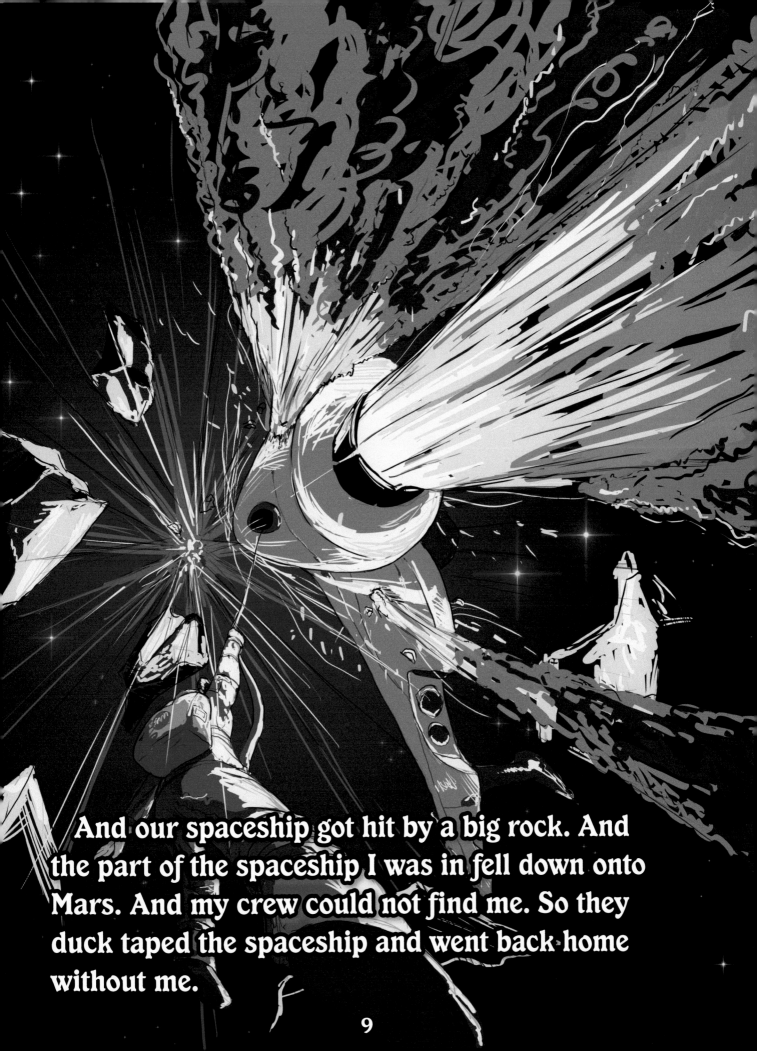

And our spaceship got hit by a big rock. And the part of the spaceship I was in fell down onto Mars. And my crew could not find me. So they duck taped the spaceship and went back home without me.

I was lost on planet mars. I found an old space station where I stayed warm and waited for someone to come find me. No one came so I had to do something.

I started looking around and found some good snacks to eat and some water to drink then I found a flashlight yea oh what a cheer! Now I can signal back home. Help, help I am alive was my code signal.

People all over the world looked to the sky and said it's a flashing star.

My crew was at NASA repairing the spaceship when someone came running and yelling its Anthony. He is alive.

So they signaled back to him saying once you were lost and now you have been found we see the light you are a star. We are coming to get you keep flashing your light so we know where you are. Anthony's crew rushed into the spaceship to go get Anthony.

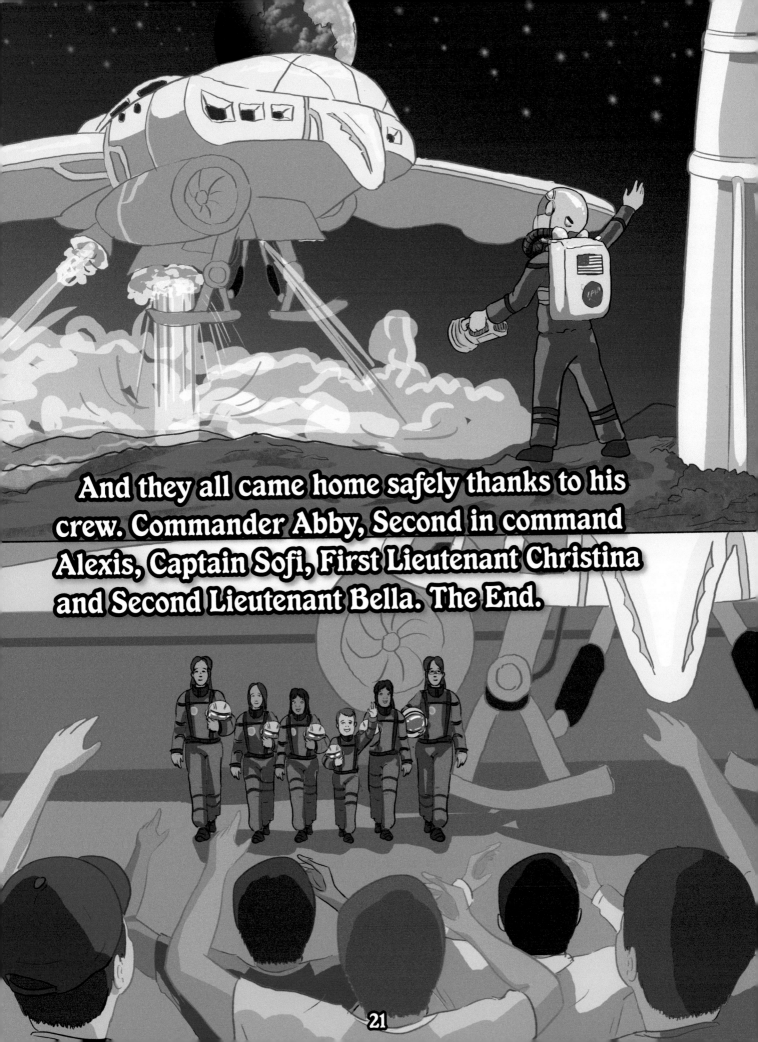

And they all came home safely thanks to his crew. Commander Abby, Second in command Alexis, Captain Sofi, First Lieutenant Christina and Second Lieutenant Bella. The End.

Printed in the United States
By Bookmasters